A WITCH COZY MYSTERY

NOVELETTE 1

T. LOCKHAVEN
CATHERINE LACROIX

<u>EDITOR</u>
GRACE LOCKHAVEN

TWISTED KEY
publishing

2024

First Printing: 2024

ISBN 978-1-63911-128-2

Twisted Key Publishing, LLC
www.twistedkeypublishing.com

Ordering Information:
Special discounts are available on quantity purchases by corporations, associations, educators, and others. For details, contact the publisher at the above listed address.

U.S. trade bookstores and wholesalers: Please contact Twisted Key Publishing, LLC by email twistedkeypublishing@gmail.com.

TABLE OF
CONTENTS

———◆———

Of all the magic Ophelia Windsor knew, there wasn't a single spell that would take care of paperwork. Which was unfortunate since paperwork was her least favorite activity in all the world. The tedium tried her patience, and having to write the same repetitive phrase line after line made her cross-eyed. She'd asked Renee once, sure that the ancient High Sorceress could offer the tiniest incantation that would move the pen on its own. But Ophelia's best friend had laughed as if she'd just heard a hilarious joke.

And so, the paperwork continued.

Ophelia adjusted her reading glasses and took a drag from her cigarette. The worst part of it all was that she'd had to bring it home to her apartment. The moon was high in the sky, slowly creeping toward the horizon in a constant reminder that she should be in bed. Sleeping.

"*Meow!*" Figaro cried as he wove his way between Ophelia's calves.

"I agree," Ophelia murmured. She wasn't the only one who wanted to sleep. Figaro was very opinionated when it came to their routine—especially when it was broken.

Figaro leapt into Ophelia's lap and walked in quick circles over her thighs. "*Meow!*" His cries grew louder, and Ophelia laid down her pen.

"Figaro? Are you alright?" She stroked his back, but the cat continued his circling. His tail stood straight up, and the tip flicked back and forth.

"*Mraow! Mrr...*" Figaro growled, then quivered.

Ophelia scooped him into her arms and stood. "Did you get into the refrigerator again? You know you're not supposed to eat my food." Not that there was a lot in there. She'd worked long hours almost every day for the last two weeks.

"Why would I not be allowed to eat from my own kitchen?" a deep, distinguished voice replied.

Ophelia spun on her heel. *An intruder?* "Who's there?" But there was no one. Just Ophelia's desk and the pile of paperwork. Her gun was in the top drawer. She stepped toward it when the voice sounded again.

"Excuse me, but I believe I'll ask the questions here!" he commanded. "Who are you? And what are you doing in my house?"

As she listened to him speak, Ophelia realized that the voice came from her arms. She looked down in disbelief. "Figaro?"

"Now you're speaking nonsense! Unhand me, wretch!"

Stunned, Ophelia knelt and placed her cat on the floor. *Am I dreaming?* But that seemed impossible. She couldn't decide whether to rush for her gun or for the mirror linked to Renee's.

"Hmm. I don't recall this room…" Figaro stalked across the floor, then looked up at Ophelia. "My, but aren't *you* large? Do you have a name, monstrous woman?"

"Ophelia Windsor," she replied. "And yours?"

Figaro threw his head back and laughed. The human gesture looked odd on his feline form. "Ah, but everyone knows me! Samuel Quentin, CEO of *Artisanal Aromas,* curator of Von Maur's top-selling fragrances!"

His introduction sounded rehearsed. But that didn't explain what the CEO of a perfume company was doing inside of her cat. "Do you often inhabit the bodies of animals, Mr. Quentin?"

"What kind of question is that?" Samuel perched on his haunches and raised a hand to his mouth, licking the fur on his paw. "I've never heard of such—" He froze, looking from his paw to an awaiting Ophelia. A catty shriek escaped his throat, and he leapt high into the air before darting from one end of the living room to the other.

"I'll take that as a 'no,'" Ophelia murmured.

"What is this foul witchcraft?" Samuel shouted. His words were punctuated by another feline screech. "This is not my estate! What have you done to me, woman? Why am I a *cat*?"

"I've done nothing to you, Mr. Quentin," Ophelia replied. "And I would very much like my cat back if you would be so kind."

"I...! How...?" He slowed to a stop at Ophelia's feet. Steady realization settled in his golden eyes, and he wrapped his tail around his chest. He stared at it like an invasive pest, and a low hiss slid between his teeth. "What's happened to me?"

Ophelia retrieved a new cigarette and lit it as she reviewed what she knew of therianthropy. However, that would have required him to shapeshift into a cat. There wasn't a second cat in Ophelia's apartment—Mr. Quentin was very much inhabiting Figaro's body.

"Why don't we try to find out together?" Ophelia asked calmly. It was too soon to call Renee—well, too late, really. Even Renee would be asleep by this hour.

"How do I know I can trust you?"

"I don't think you have much of a choice, Mr. Quentin. Besides, as I said, it's my cat you're living inside, and it would benefit us both if you weren't." A small smile twitched at the side of her mouth. "How do I know you aren't a demon? I've heard exorcisms work well for this sort of thing—"

"How dare you?! A demon? I am one of the most powerful men in Illinois!" His tail rocked back and forth in angry ticks.

"It was a joke," Ophelia replied. At least she had his ear.

"…This is not a time for jests, *Ophelia.*"

"Ms. Windsor, if you'd be so kind." Ophelia flicked a bit of ash away from the tip of her cigarette. "Are you an immortal, Mr. Quentin?"

"What kind of question is that?" Something like a scoff arranged itself on Samuel's face. "I believe I am very much mortal like the rest of us."

So he's not in the circle. That was too bad. An immortal already aware of their powers or heritage would have been an easier start. Explaining magic to an unknowing human was… arduous, at best.

"I do not like this. Staring up at you." He looked from side to side, then turned to find her sofa. He pounced toward the back, overshot, and faceplanted into the cushions. "Say nothing!" Ophelia hid a smile behind another long pull of her cigarette as Samuel rearranged himself on the sofa's backing. "There. Much better. Now. Where were we?"

"Diagnosing your situation. Are you a lucid dreamer?" Ophelia asked.

"I beg your pardon?"

"When you dream, do you find that you can control what's happening or influence what occurs next?" Ophelia explained. "For example, while in your dream you picture yourself flying, and then you do fly."

"I suppose sometimes, yes. But I imagine that everyone can do that." He straightened his back and pawed at the sofa's fabric. "Are you saying that I'm dreaming?"

Ophelia shrugged. "There's a chance that you're what's called a wanderer. A person who detaches their consciousness when they dream."

Samuel blinked. The hair on his neck stood up. "Ms. Windsor, who *are* you, exactly?"

"I'm a private investigator."

"A private investigator who questions immortality and suggests impossible feats like *detaching myself from my body*?" He tilted his head to the side.

Ophelia hesitated. On the one hand, there was an excellent chance that Samuel had accidentally tapped into a resource of magic he hadn't realized he held. Many latent immortals realized their powers on their own, without the help of their parents. But if he woke up the next morning back in his own body knowing of the circle, the immortals, and Ophelia's being a witch, even the tiniest seed of doubt could put them all in danger before she could find him.

On the other hand, if he was under the effects of a spell, this could be a more permanent situation. At that point, knowing that magic was, in fact, very real could help calm him.

I really need Renee. This wasn't a decision to make lightly, and Renee was the head of the immortal circle in Cicero. There wouldn't be a better person to ask.

"Hello? Are you still with me?" Samuel turned to lick his back, paused, and then gagged. "Why do I have such a terrible urging to do that?"

"That's Figaro's spirit conflicting with yours," Ophelia said. "Look, Mr. Quentin. I have a friend who may be able to help us. My suggestion for the night is that we both sleep on this. Best case scenario, you'll wake up at home in your own bed. Worst case, we get her help in the morning."

Samuel bowed his head. "I must stay a cat?"

"Just until I can figure out what's going on." Ophelia finished her cigarette and dashed the filter against the ashtray. As much as she would miss Figaro's warm company, she wasn't comfortable inviting a stranger into her room. "I can get you a blanket, and you can sleep on the couch."

"I am quite warm, thank you." The authoritative tone vanished, replaced by a begrudging acceptance. "All of this fur does well at keeping the heat in, at least."

"Keep your chin up, Mr. Quentin. You chose a good cat to inhabit."

He groaned, though it sounded more like a purr, then jumped down onto the cushions. Ophelia glanced at her paperwork, then at the clock. It was nearing three a.m., and her mind spun while attempting to understand Samuel's predicament.

She fell asleep with the wish that Figaro would be himself again in the morning.

Figaro's paws kneaded Ophelia's hair shortly before her alarm clock sounded.

"Figaro, you're up so early," Ophelia grumbled.

"Have you forgotten already?" snapped the cat. "Hmph. Some detective you are."

Gangbusters. "No, Mr. Quentin, I did not." *So much for my wish.* Ophelia sighed. "By the way, it's rude to enter a lady's room without knocking."

Samuel laughed incredulously. "You expect me to knock? With paws?"

"Not one for humor, are you?" Ophelia yawned and switched off her clock.

"This. Is not. Funny!"

The phone rang, startling them both.

"Your friend, I presume?" Samuel asked.

Ophelia slid from the warmth of her bed and pushed her bare feet into the awaiting slippers. "She usually isn't up this early." She shuffled to the phone and lifted the receiver. "Hello?"

"Ophelia. It's Lieutenant Jackson."

That wasn't good. If Jackson couldn't leave a message with Julia or Tiffany at the office, that meant it was urgent. She eyed Samuel as he padded toward her. "What can I do for you, Jackson?"

"There's been an… incident," Jackson said slowly.

"A murder?"

"I can't say that on record yet. But Detective Frisbe's asked for you personally."

Ophelia furrowed her brow. Donald Frisbe had never cared for her methods and always saw her work as 'snooping around.' For him to request her didn't make sense. "Why?"

"He wants a second opinion. Outside of the force."

Well, that was interesting. Donald Frisbe was a man who played by the books. But he didn't know of the arcane, the immortals, or the circle. "Was Officer Brewer at the scene?" It was an easier way to ask a very superstitious lieutenant if an immortal had already looked it over.

"She was. She didn't find anything." Jackson huffed. "I've got another call coming in. Can you humor the detective or not?"

Ophelia looked at Samuel, then at the clock. Renee wouldn't be up for a few hours anyway. "Sure, Jackson." She collected her pen and notepad from beside the phone and flipped open the cover. "What's the address?"

He rattled it off with a curt goodbye, and Ophelia replaced the receiver. She lifted it one more time to dial the operator and request a cab, then set it down for good. "Samuel, I need to look into this. Think you can hold down the fort?"

"Excuse me? What of your friend? What of my body?"

"It'll be the first thing we do when I get back. A few more hours like this won't hurt your chances of restoring you where you belong. Scout's honor." Ophelia flipped her notebook shut and moved to her room.

"How can you be so sure? How do you know all of these things?" Samuel trotted beside her, the fur on his paws tickling her heels.

"You have to trust me." Ophelia shut her bedroom door before Samuel could come in with her and quickly dressed. "I'll explain everything once I get back."

"This is ludicrous! I have never had to wait for anything!" Samuel mewled from behind the door. "Do you not understand who I am? Who I know?"

Ophelia smirked. She could say the same. "I understand that you're upset. This won't take long, Mr. Quentin."

A frustrated snarl followed in response and then silence. Ophelia left the room and snatched her coat from the tall wooden stand in her doorway. "There's food in your dish. I'll pick up some tuna on the way home."

"Unbelievable! You demand I consume cat food?"

Her fridge was empty. As it usually was. "Well, I may have a little milk."

Samuel scratched his ear with his back paw. "Nothing else? Just cat food and *a little milk*?"

She shook her head and marched to her phone. The sooner she had Figaro back, the better. "Let me try and call Renee."

"Preposterous." Samuel pounced toward the food dish and inhaled. "This cat food is dry! What kind of heathen purchases dry cat food?"

"It wasn't by choice." Figaro wouldn't touch the wet stuff. Ophelia spun the dial on her phone, entering Renee's number in a few quick sweeps. She wasn't ready to show Samuel her mirror. Not yet. Finding himself in the body of a cat was already taking its toll. Explaining a magic mirror before she went to find Frisbe would be impossible.

The phone rang once. Twice. Thrice. Then clicked over to Renee's answering machine.

Ophelia sighed and replaced the receiver. Renee often slept right through a ringing phone;

the only surefire way to reach her now was the mirror.

"Mr. Quentin, I promise we'll call my friend again when I return. And you won't need to suffer the cat food long."

"I refuse to eat it at all! What a dreadful host you are, Ms. Windsor! If it were me—"

Ophelia closed the door before she heard another word.

The cab was waiting for her when she left the apartment building. Max stood at the back door, holding it open for her with a grin.

"Good morning, Ms. Windsor!"

"You're up early, Max," Ophelia greeted.

"Ah, well, little Suzy's got me and the missus working graveyards." Max winked. His daughter was barely a few months old, but Max was ever the glowing father. "I'm hoping I can give Nancy the night to sleep."

"That's very considerate of you." Ophelia stepped inside the cab, and he closed the door behind her. At least there was one bright face she could count on during the very strange morning.

Max slipped into the driver's seat and started the taxi. "Where to this fine morning?"

Ophelia read the address from her notepad, and Max nodded his affirmation. She filled the space with idle conversation and rolled down the window just a crack. She'd missed out on her usual morning coffee, and after staying up so late the night prior, sleep crept in at the edges of her vision.

At last, the cab rolled to a halt outside of a set of enormous golden gates with two lions fashioned in their center. The left one was already propped open by about a foot, and Ophelia could see police cars in the distance.

"Golly. Nothing like the smell of old money in the morning," Max murmured.

"You can say that again." Ophelia handed him a few folded bills. "Mind waiting for me, Max?"

Max accepted the fold and grinned. "Never, Ms. Windsor."

"Your secret's safe with me if you want to sneak in a nap," Ophelia said as she stepped out of the cab. Max offered her a good-natured salute, and she walked through the gate.

The house came into view as Ophelia traversed the smooth, paved road. Though, 'house' was not the correct term—not by a long shot. This was an *estate*; a mansion like the castles and well-to-do properties that Renee owned in the quiet corners of Europe. Towering columns held up the roof of a two-story house with eight windows spanning its exterior. Manicured gardens with rare flowers and sculpted bushes decorated the front lawn, entertaining visitors from the moment they entered the golden gates.

Detective Frisbe stood at the front door. His thin brown belt was pulled tight beneath the slight paunch of his stomach, and his wide mustache was waxed tightly against his face. The twin panels of oak housed stained glass designs inside their frames and sported brass gargoyle knockers and elegant handles. Sweat beaded on Donald's brow, and he adjusted his tie with trembling hands.

"Good morning, Detective Frisbe," Ophelia greeted cordially, though she still didn't understand why he'd requested her. They'd never been unkind to one another, per se, but there was always a certain tension that arose between them when matched on the same case.

"Ms. Windsor," Detective Frisbe said. He rubbed his palms against the thighs of his gray tweed suit. "Thank you for coming."

"Of course." Ophelia looked over her shoulder and lowered her voice. "Lieutenant Jackson didn't give me much on what's going on here. I apologize, but you'll have to fill me in."

"Certainly. Please, follow me."

Ophelia tried to recall if he'd ever been so cordial with her but came up blank. Something about this case really bothered him.

They entered through the double doors into a high-ceilinged foyer featuring more columns, a slew of sculptures on decorative marble blocks, and original artwork hung on the walls. *This place would give Renee a run for her money.* More lions were artfully hidden throughout their walk—painted inside the wallpaper's trim, inside a few of the paintings they passed, and engraved into various ashtrays and cigar boxes.

"So, what happened here, Detective?" Ophelia asked. Her boots clicked against the ivory tile, and the silence crawled over her skin.

"On the record? A man died of a heart failure last night," Detective Frisbe said quietly.

"And off the record?"

There was a long pause, and then Detective Frisbe said, "I believe he was murdered."

"Oh?" Despite them both keeping their voices low, they echoed against the high ceilings and spacious rooms with the perfect acoustics of a concert hall.

"It just doesn't make any sense to me," Detective Frisbe continued. "I have a few calls out to his physicians. But I spoke to his general practitioner this morning, who saw him two weeks ago. Clean bill of health—no complaints of chest pain or otherwise."

"To play devil's advocate, Detective, sudden medical onsets happen all the time," Ophelia countered. It was something she'd seen over her few hundred years of existence. Sometimes, science just wasn't enough to determine the mysteries of the human body. "Maybe the doctor didn't run the right tests."

"Maybe. And that's something I'll readily accept." Detective Frisbe ran a hand through his hair. It was absent of the heavy gel he usually applied to his locks. "But the victim just launched a new line of product that was *booming*. We're talking millions of dollars in profits. The timing of his death feels... a little too perfect."

"Alright. Allow me to take a few steps back. Who's our victim here, Detective?"

"One Mr. Quentin," Detective Frisbe said without checking his notes. "Samuel Quentin."

3

Ophelia froze mid-step. "Samuel Quentin? The perfume magnate?"

Detective Frisbe nodded. "One and the same. You've heard of him?"

"Er, yes, hasn't everyone?" Ophelia attempted a casual laugh, but it fell flat. She cleared her throat and forced herself to keep walking. "He's dead?"

"In the morgue as we speak, Ms. Windsor. As I said, the first diagnosis this morning was heart failure."

"No evidence of foul play?"

"Nothing. No external wounds and no blood where they found him. We'll have to wait on autopsy results for stomach contents—so, for now, poison is still on the table. But the medical examiner has his doubts."

Samuel's dead spirit was haunting Ophelia's cat. And he had no idea that he was dead. *This just got a lot more complicated.* "Isn't this something the police department would handle? Especially if everything points to a natural death?"

"Typically, yes. I have a strong feeling that they'll examine him, find the cause to be heart failure, and close the books on this one." Detective Frisbe stopped by a polished door with a golden nametag emblazoned across its front. *Samuel Quentin.* He pushed open the door to a room filled with wood shelves and a mahogany desk, then closed the door when Ophelia stepped through. Everything was dust-free and well-organized. Books were arranged in alphabetical order, and every pen and paper had a specific place on the desk. A mosaic on the floor depicted a lion on its hind legs, roaring at the sky. Behind it were two crossed flags— one red, one gold.

"Jackson won't pursue this case. I know that; you know that. So, please, I'm asking as a favor. Check this one out," Detective Frisbe pleaded.

"You want to hire me on a hunch?" Ophelia crossed her arms and peered around the room. The truth was, she was more than ready to accept the case. Samuel deserved to know what had happened to him, and she agreed with the detective—there was more to this than met the eye.

But she had to make Detective Frisbe struggle a little bit. If not for vanity's sake.

"I know this sounds crazy, but I'll be able to sleep a lot better at night if you investigate this case and then tell me I've lost my marbles,"

Detective Frisbe said. "I'll owe you one—" Ophelia narrowed her gaze; this was one heck of a favor, "—okay, more than one. But you can still investigate suspects and find your own way around. I've seen you do it before. If I try to do my own digging, Jackson'll tan my hide."

That was true. Jackson was far stricter on the rules than Detective Frisbe. Ophelia would be lucky to escape his ire for pressing the matter. But with Samuel's ghost haunting her apartment, there were a lot of questions that needed to be answered. She made a show of relenting. "Alright. Okay. I'll look into it."

Detective Frisbe smiled, and the tension evaporated from his shoulders. "Thank you so much, Ms. Windsor. I'm in your debt—"

"I'll hold you to that." She gestured to the desk. "So, are we hiding here in secret? Or did you bring me to Mr. Quentin's office for a reason?"

"This is where his assistant found his body. Right where you're standing."

Ophelia looked around her feet. No blood. Nothing seemed disturbed or out of place in terms of books or the effects on his desk. *It's as if he just dropped dead.* "His assistant comes to his house?"

"Every morning, apparently."

Ophelia nodded. "Any other suspects?"

His smile widened, and he fished his notebook from his jacket pocket. "Three, in fact. The estate's workers were very helpful."

"Did you find any of the workers suspicious?" Ophelia mirrored him and pulled her own notebook from her coat.

"Personally, no. The three I'm giving you have more to gain from his death than those he employed." Detective Frisbe shrugged. "But you're free to check in with them."

"I'll keep that in mind." Ophelia flipped open the top and readied her pen. "Alright. Names. Shoot."

"First is Clara Quentin, Samuel's wife. I think the potential motive on this one was pretty clear."

It was. "Is Clara still here?"

"Right upstairs. She's a tough nut to crack."

Ophelia nodded and scribbled Clara's name down. "Next?"

"Edward Albrecht, Samuel's business partner. They've run the *Artisanal Aromas* operation together since its inception. Their company will be rewritten in his name, as well as all of its assets."

Another solid motive. "Where can I reach him?"

Detective Frisbe read off the address and phone number for the offices of *Artisanal Aromas.*

Ophelia nodded. "And last?"

"The final suspect is Victoria LaCoste. Samuel's assistant and the one who discovered his body."

Ophelia penned Victoria's name, then hovered over it. "Is that the only reason she's a suspect?"

"This one's a little fuzzy, but," Detective Frisbe rounded Samuel's desk and lifted a picture frame, turning it to face Ophelia, "something tells me they were close."

A tall, stocky man and a thin young woman stood on a yacht, arms around one another's waists. He had a full head of salt-and-pepper hair, and the buttons on his expensive suit jacket were holding on for dear life. The woman's dark hair was elegantly styled, and she wore light makeup with her wiggle dress. Each held a glass of sparkling wine in one hand, and they wore warm smiles. "Is this Samuel and Victoria?"

"It is. If you need extra assurance, 'S & V 1955' is written on the bottom corner."

"Mind if I take that picture?" Ophelia pocketed her notebook and held out one hand.

"No. Just make sure it comes home when you're finished." Detective Frisbe carefully removed the frame's backing and pulled the photo free.

Ophelia added it to the same pocket as her notebook, careful to position it where it wouldn't be bent or creased. "Anything else?"

"That's all I have right now." He slipped his notes into his jacket and readjusted his tie. "I mean it, Ms. Windsor, if heart failure's the real cause of death here, nothing would make me happier."

"Why do you say that like you have a dog in this fight, Mr. Frisbe?"

"No dogs. It's just…" He shivered and pulled his coat close. Avoiding her gaze, he stepped past her and opened the office door. "Nothing feels right about this case. I hope you'll tell me I'm wrong."

Detective Frisbe left Ophelia alone in the office. She briefly wondered how she would break the news of Samuel's death to him when she returned home before beginning her search for Clara Quentin.

'Upstairs' was a painfully general term when the winding staircase seemed to ascend for miles. Outside, Ophelia had counted windows that suggested a two-story house.

Inside, it felt like she was working her way to the next state over.

At last, she reached the top, where two police officers exited a room far down the opulent hallway. One of them was Cynthia Brewer—a specialist in physical magics. She lingered behind as her partner started down the staircase, nodding her greeting to Ophelia.

"Good morning, Officer Brewer," Ophelia said. "Nothing out of place?"

Cynthia shook her head. "Not a book, not a hair, not a throw pillow." She lowered her voice. "No wards, no protections, and no barriers. This place is as clean as a whistle."

"Thank you."

"Of course, Ms. Windsor. Just doing my duty." She tipped her hat. "But, if you don't mind me asking, why were you called in? This case seems pretty black and white."

"Well, that's what I'm hoping for—an easy case." Ophelia wasn't ready to talk about Samuel the cat. Not when his wife was in earshot. "I'll keep Jackson updated."

"I'll keep an ear to the ground, then. Have a good day, Ms. Windsor."

"You too, Officer Brewer."

They went their separate ways, and Ophelia strode toward the door the officers had occupied. More art, potted flowers, and sculptures lined the hallway, and the white double doors at the end were opened just a crack. She knocked on the left door and waited.

"Come in," called a soft, feminine voice.

Ophelia stepped inside. A woman in her early forties with burgundy hair and puffy hazel eyes sat in a fur-trimmed robe at the edge of her four-poster bed. She cuddled a pillow to her stomach and dabbed her cheeks with a tissue. A Persian rug covered the thick carpet from the doorway to the bed, and Ophelia inched around it. One misstep on that piece would cost her a few months of pay.

"Mrs. Quentin?" Ophelia asked as she made it to a safe area to stand.

"Who else?" Clara sputtered. Her eyes darted to Ophelia's feet, and she heaved a sigh of relief. "At least you have taste. There have been unwelcome boots trampling my carpets all morning."

Have you forgotten about Samuel already? "I'm Ophelia Windsor, ma'am. I'd like to ask you a few questions."

"I was told there would be no further questioning!" Clara sniffed and glowered at Ophelia.

"While your cooperation with the police is immensely appreciated, I'm a private investigator, ma'am."

Clara's features darkened. "And who hired you? Hm?"

The police. Ophelia straightened her back and retrieved her notebook. Donald was right; Clara would be a tough nut to crack. "Mrs. Quentin, what's important is that we find the truth behind your husband's death and clear all names if possible."

"Clear names?" Clara raised her penciled brows. "Are you saying this was a *murder*?"

"I can't say either way. I'm hoping you can assist me with that."

"Sam was on a dozen medications! His heart was weak, and he ate everything he could fit into his pudgy little mouth. Is it really such a shock that his terrible habits finally caught up with him?"

Ophelia noted the medications, hoping Detective Frisbe could fill in the names for her once he heard from Samuel's doctors. "When was the last time you saw Samuel, Mrs. Quentin?"

"Yesterday afternoon before I went out."

"And where were you last night?"

"Like I told the police," Clara said sharply, "I was running a charity event at the town hall from four o'clock to ten o'clock." She touched the tissue to her nose.

"A charity event for what?"

"For Save the Children. I run a chapter in Cicero." Clara shook her head. "Sam spent his life drowning the world in luxury and perfume. I wanted to do my best to counteract his one-track mind and give back to the less fortunate of us."

Unhappy marriage, Ophelia scribbled into her book. "Did you not see him when you came home?"

"I rarely saw him in the evenings. He locked himself in his office with a cigar and his gramophone every night. His truest loves."

Clara was dancing around the problem—a problem that painted a solid motive. Ophelia wanted to pin it down as soon as possible. "So you didn't expect him here? In your bedroom?"

Clara whisked her hair over one shoulder, though the flick of her wrist seemed to bat away Ophelia's question. "We haven't shared this room in quite some time."

"Were you and Samuel not on good terms, Mrs. Quentin?"

"What a personal question to ask. Doesn't every marriage have its issues, Mrs. Windsor?"

"I wouldn't know."

A sardonic smile curled Clara's lips. "Aren't you a lucky gal, then?" She tossed the pillow aside and stood, pulling the satin robe closer to her slim form. "Of course we had our ups and downs, but I made vows I planned to stand beside. Fate seems to have cut that short." She wriggled her fingers at Ophelia. "And you can write all that down on your little notepad."

Ophelia chewed her tongue as she stared at her notes, carefully considering the next question she should ask. "Is there anyone who would have wanted to cause him harm?"

Clara laughed. It was a high, practiced sound like tinkling bells. "Oh, goodness. You must not understand what comes with power, Ms. Windsor." She covered her mouth with one dainty hand and leveled her gaze with Ophelia's. "When you have an empire like Samuel's, you have many, many friends. And just as many enemies." Her smile returned. "However, this time, I believe Samuel's adversary was himself."

Ophelia nodded. "What do you know of Victoria LaCoste?"

Anger flashed in Clara's eyes. "She played Sam's assistant."

Played? "Does she not work in Samuel's office?"

"Oh, she does. And she works here. And wherever else he asked her to be."

"So her appearance this morning was typical?"

"That is certainly a word for it."

Possible affair, Ophelia wrote. It seemed there wasn't much else she'd be able to get out of Clara. "Thank you very much for your time, Mrs. Quentin."

"Hm." Clara lifted a prescription bottle from her nightstand and popped the cap. "Good luck with your investigation, Ms. Windsor."

Ophelia excused herself, tiptoeing around the rug, before confronting the never-ending staircase once again. Clara's agitated disposition with her deceased husband was suspicious, but it wasn't the first time Ophelia had encountered an estranged, dissatisfied spouse. Whether it was enough for Clara to commit murder was yet to be seen.

When she made it to the bottom floor, Ophelia found her way through the expansive hallways to the backyard, hoping Victoria hadn't left the estate yet. Thankfully, she found the young woman hunched over on one of the many pool chairs surrounding an Olympic-sized pool.

Victoria's brunette hair fell over her shoulders in tight curls, but her face was hidden as she cried quietly into her hands. She wore a tight-fitting jacket and a long skirt with a pair of matching black heels. A leather purse leaned against the pool chair's leg beside a discarded jacket and pair of gloves.

"Ms. LaCoste?" Ophelia called, taking a seat on the pool chair beside Victoria.

"Y-yes?" Victoria lowered her hands, revealing a face smeared with makeup. "My apologies, I've made a mess of myself." With a sad laugh, she retrieved her purse and fished out a cloth handkerchief. "I'm Victoria LaCoste."

"Ophelia Windsor." Ophelia readied her notepad.

"Are you with the police?"

"No. I'm a private investigator. I've been asked to look into Samuel Quentin's death."

Fresh tears gathered in the corners of Victoria's eyes, and her lower lip trembled. "I kept telling Sam he needed to eat better. Get off all those medications. He… I…" A new wave of sobs overtook her words, and she collected her tears in her handkerchief.

"It sounds like you and Mr. Quentin were close."

"I was his personal assistant. But it was so much more than that, Ms. Windsor. We understood each other and could anticipate what the other needed. He wasn't just my boss; he was my dearest friend."

Ophelia underlined 'Possible affair' twice. "Do you always begin your day at this residence, Ms. LaCoste?"

"Yes." Victoria sniffed. "He wanted to improve his diet—his doctor suggested the same. The chefs he hired catered too much to what he asked. So, I made him breakfast each morning."

"How long have you been doing that?"

"Um, years now. At least four or five." Victoria reached for her purse. "I can check my planner for the exact date if you need. Anything I can do to help."

"I don't believe that's necessary, Ms. LaCoste. Can you tell me what happened this morning?"

"Well, like I told the police, I arrived at six a.m. like I usually do and went to start his breakfast in the kitchen."

"Was anyone else in the house?"

"Not yet. In the mornings, they usually keep one chef on duty—Franklin—for Mrs. Quentin's breakfast and lunch and then a housekeeper, Beverly. Franklin's shift starts at seven, and Beverly was running late. So, it was just me."

"Does that mean you have your own key to the house?"

"I do. Mr. and Mrs. Quentin like to sleep in until six-thirty or seven."

Ophelia made a note. "What happened after you arrived?"

"I went to the kitchen to get started, but I heard the sound of a record scratching in Sam's office. He never leaves the gramophone on, so I went in to check. T-that's when I... I..." Tears spilled down her cheeks, and she took a deep breath. "I found him on the floor. Just lying there."

"Mrs. Quentin wasn't awake yet?"

"No. No, it was just me and... and Sam."

"Were you the one who called the police?"

Victoria opened her mouth to reply, then nodded instead.

Ophelia frowned and took a deep breath. "Ms. LaCoste, there's never an easy way to ask this, but were you and Mr. Quentin having an affair?"

Victoria's eyes widened, and she gaped, a horrified expression settling into her features. "No! I would never do such a thing to Mrs. Quentin!" She shook her head so quickly that her hair bounced from side to side with the motion. "They've been nothing but kind and generous to me. To even *imagine* such a thing..." She touched her chest and looked up at the sky. "I couldn't. I can't."

"Of course. Thank you." It was either a very good act, or Victoria was telling the truth. Ophelia hoped she could corroborate it with Samuel. Although a cat's facial expressions would be much more challenging to read. "How long have you worked for the Quentins?"

"Goodness, a little over a decade. They're like family to me."

Dearest friend to family. "Do you have any family in Cicero, Ms. LaCoste?"

"No. It's just little old me here. My mother lives in Massachusetts. I moved this way with an old boyfriend, but he's long gone." Victoria looked down at her lap. "I would have gone back, but I love my job and my life here."

"That's understandable. Can you please tell me where you were last night?"

"Actually, that's a little embarrassing." She coughed up a weak laugh. "I was out of town the last few days visiting my mother. She's been sick and needs surgery soon. I returned early this morning and came straight to work."

"I'm sorry to hear that. Why do you find that embarrassing?"

"I think most daughters would move home if their mothers were in such a condition. But I don't think Sam can manage more than a few days without me." Victoria blushed. "I'd feel dreadful if anything were to happen to him."

"I see. Your mother can confirm you were with her?"

"Yes, absolutely."

"Do you have your flight information, by chance?"

Victoria pulled her planner from her purse. "I do. And here's my mother's phone number."

Ophelia accepted both and added them to her notepad. Satisfied, she retrieved a business card from her coat pocket and passed it forward. "If you think of anything at all, could you give me a call at this number, please?"

"Oh. Yes! Of course!" Victoria accepted the card and slid it into her purse. "Thank you, Ms. Windsor. Sam meant a lot to so many people. He deserves only the best."

"You're welcome. I'll contact you if I need any further information. Please take care, Ms. LaCoste."

"You, too, Ms. Windsor."

Ophelia left Victoria alone and went back into the house. She stopped one of the three housekeepers rushing about the rooms and asked to use their phone. After she guided her to one in the foyer, she contemplated who to call first. She needed Renee to examine Samuel with her and determine the best course for freeing his spirit from Figaro's body. But she also wanted to meet with Edward Albrecht and solidify Victoria and Clara's alibis.

The image of Samuel eating dried cat food won out over all three. She dialed Renee Swan's number from memory.

Renee answered on the third ring. "Hello?"

"Renee. It's Ophelia."

"Oh, darling, the phone again?" Renee yawned. "Our mirrors are so much more convenient."

"While I agree, I'm not at home at the moment. I was hoping you could meet me there in, say," Ophelia checked her watch, "half an hour?"

"My, my. This must be urgent," Renee mused. "Of course I can. Anything for you, my sweet."

"Thank you, Renee. I'll be there soon." Ophelia hung up and thanked the housekeeper for her time.

She made her way outside, down the paved road, and to the front gates. The police cars were absent, and the investigating officers had gone with them. Max's cab waited patiently for her return, with a napping Max in the front seat. Ophelia grinned and softly knocked on the window. Max blinked three times and yawned, then registered that she was standing outside waiting for him. In a panic, he jumped out of the cab and opened the back seat.

"I did say you could nap, Max," Ophelia teased.

"And I owe you my thanks, Ms. Windsor! It perked me right up." Max straightened his shoulders and closed the door behind her before retaking the front seat. "Where to?"

"Let's stop by the store on our way back to my apartment, Max." Ophelia found her pack of cigarettes and extracted one from the carton. "I need to feed my cat."

4

When Ophelia stepped off the elevator, Renee was already waiting at her apartment door. The High Sorceress's auburn hair was braided back in intricate knots and bedecked with tiny gemstones that sparkled in the dim hallway. Her deep green gown and ivory fur coat were fit for a fancy soirée rather than a trip to a friend's apartment. But Ophelia had long since given up on telling her that.

"Ophelia, darling! Pray forgive my appearance. This was the best I could do in so little time." Renee grasped Ophelia's shoulders and kissed her cheek.

"Took the words right out of my mouth, Renee." Ophelia smiled. "I believe this will be easier if I just… show you."

"Oh, how exciting! I do love a good mystery."

Ophelia fished her keys from her pocket and unlocked her apartment door.

"It's about time!" Samuel shouted from the sofa. "You're starving me to death on purpose, aren't you?"

"A man?" Renee wiggled her eyebrows, and a playful smile tugged at her mouth.

"Nothing that salacious," Ophelia murmured, taking the can of tuna from the grocery bag as she crossed the living room to the kitchen.

"A second voice? Is that your friend I hear?" Samuel hopped over the couch and sat back to scratch his ear.

"Figaro can speak!" Renee cried. "Well, I'll be! How did you manage such a difficult spell on your own, sweet?"

"This isn't Figaro. This is Samuel Quentin." Ophelia freed the tuna with a can opener and went to set it down for Samuel.

Renee had crouched down beside Samuel, who fixed his yellow eyes on her beautiful face.

"Pardonnez-moi, ma dame! Je n'ai jamais vu une telle beauté," Samuel purred.

Ophelia rolled her eyes. Everyone liked Renee. Even Detective Frisbe. She always wondered if they'd like her as much if they knew what the High Sorceress was capable of.

"Oh, how sweet! *Tu es pardonné, cher chat.*" Renee scratched Samuel's neck, and his eyes closed. "What a delightful house guest you've made, Ophelia."

"*Pour toi, il est,*" Ophelia grumbled. She slid the tuna toward Samuel and took a seat on the carpet. "Here. Eat."

Samuel's eyes snapped open, and he darted for the tuna, then stopped. "*This* is the best you can give me?"

"I can't feed you anything that will hurt Figaro, Mr. Quentin. And, by association, hurt you."

Samuel hissed, but he licked at the canned fish anyway. His gaze lit up at the first taste, and he quickly devoured the rest.

"So, my dear, how did this come to pass?" Renee asked as she stared at Samuel in wonder.

Ophelia explained Samuel's sudden appearance the previous evening. She was certain that Figaro's spirit was still residing in the same body since she observed multiple cat-like instincts coming to the forefront.

"How fascinating! You are certain that you do not possess the abilities of a wanderer, Samuel?"

Samuel licked his lips. "I see we've returned to the 'abilities' and 'powers' guessing game," he said sourly.

"I promised I would explain, so here you are. I'm a witch, and Renee is a High Sorceress," Ophelia replied.

He looked between them, then laughed. "This all must be a big joke, and I'm the butt of it, right? Someone set me up?"

"In that, I'm afraid you might be right." Ophelia softened her tone. "Mr. Quentin, I was called in to investigate a possible murder this morning."

"Do I know them?" Samuel asked.

"Yes. It's you. You're dead, Mr. Quentin."

Samuel's feline mouth dropped open, and every hair on his back stood on end. "W... What?"

"Oh, no," Renee whispered. "How awful."

"The first responders and medical examiner believe you died of heart failure," Ophelia continued. "I was asked to verify this."

He looked back and forth between them. "Is it because of this? Because I'm now somehow in a cat's body?"

"Wanderers leave their physical bodies in a type of stasis. Typically either meditative or by sleeping," Renee explained gently. "If your physical body has perished, then this is likely another cause."

"I... But..." Samuel fumbled for words.

"You may be predisposed to a feline aspect. I do recall a very powerful Quentin family many years ago with a lion on their crest," Renee continued.

"With two flags? That crest is in Samuel's office," Ophelia added.

"Yes, that's the one." Renee scratched behind Samuel's ear. "In my experience, your predicament could be attributed to a few spells. However, if what Ophelia says is true and this is, in fact, a murder, your spirit may have simply clung to this plane for resolution. You just so happened to find the luckiest cat alive."

Samuel melted into a black puddle of fur on the carpet. "I can't be dead... I can't..."

"I understand this is a lot to take in, but the sooner I can find out what happened, the better off we'll all be." Ophelia pulled her notebook from her pocket. "Can I ask you a few questions, Mr. Quentin?"

"Why not? What else do I have to lose?" Samuel grumbled.

"Cheer up, sweet. Things are not so terrible! Your spirit could have been caught in eternal limbo with no hope of redemption instead," Renee said.

I don't think that's helping. The disgusted look on Samuel's face said the same.

Ophelia cleared her throat. "Can you tell me everything you did yesterday?"

"Sure. I woke up at seven a.m. like I usually do. Victoria was out of town, so I had Franklin make me breakfast. Oh, Victoria's my assistant. She's usually the one that makes breakfast for me."

"She told me. You can continue."

"As you wish. I had breakfast with my wife and then went to the office. My partner, Edward, and I just released a new perfume, so work's been a blur of phone calls and handshakes. I had dinner at Rabbit's, and when I returned home, I did my usual routine."

"Which is?" Ophelia pressed.

"I go to my office, play some jazz on the gramophone, sort through the rest of my paperwork, take my pills, and have a cigar. Every man has a routine." Samuel finally straightened back to sitting and licked his paw. "The last thing I remember was hearing Ava Dean's sweet voice."

"There was no one in the office with you at the time?"

"Not that I recall."

"And you don't remember going to bed?" Ophelia clarified.

"I do not."

"There is a chance that your consciousness erased the memory of your death from your mind," Renee suggested. "Spirits cling to visions that bring them joy and reject those that give them pain. If there was, in fact, an intruder inside your office, it is likely that you will not recall it."

"Aces," Samuel groaned.

"Pardon me for asking, Samuel, but have you borne witness to anything unusual from your wife or assistant? Perhaps strange markings in the house, odd smells, or books in unrecognizable languages?" Renee asked.

"The only strange papers in my house were the terms of our divorce," Samuel grumbled.

"Divorce?" Ophelia flipped to her notes with Clara. "Mrs. Quentin didn't mention a divorce."

"No? It was her idea!" Samuel snapped. "Clara served me the papers two months ago, and she's clawing at every dime she can get." He blinked and wrinkled his nose, his whiskers twitching from side to side. "Did *Clara* do this?"

"That's certainly a strong motive," Ophelia admitted. "She claimed to have been at a charity event last night?"

"Save the Children. Yes. Clara's altruistic attempt at winning the hearts of her highfalutin peers. I didn't hear her return home, but I do play the gramophone quite loud," Samuel explained.

"Do you know by what means she could have harmed you, Samuel?" Renee asked.

"Who knows? Maybe she's a witch!" He barked an incredulous laugh.

"I highly doubt that, Mr. Quentin," Ophelia replied. "Does anyone else handle your cigars?"

"My cigar was procured from an unopened box last night. I had been saving it for a special occasion. As much as I wish I could say she did, I can't imagine Clara having the foresight to tamper with it and make it appear unused."

"Alright." Ophelia made a note beneath Clara's name. "Let's talk about Ms. LaCoste. Were you two intimately involved?"

"No. I was trying to save my marriage, Ms. Windsor, not burn what was left of it to ash." Samuel stretched his hind legs, and Renee stroked his back. He shivered. "Goodness, you certainly know how to pet a cat."

Renee giggled and scratched his tail.

Ophelia pressed on. "You said she was out of town. Do you know why?"

"Yes. Her mother's taken ill. I paid for her trip to Massachusetts and compensated her for her time off."

"You two seem very close," Renee noted.

"Clara and I never had children; Victoria's like a daughter to me. She comes from a humble background, and her mother is her only remaining family," Samuel said. "To be candid, Clara, Victoria, and Edward are the only beneficiaries in my will."

That's motive enough for all three of them. "I'd like to ask about Edward Albrecht if I could. How long have you worked together?"

"Since *Artisanal Aromas*'s inception twenty years ago. It started as a small business venture, and thanks to Edward's ties with Von Maur, our brand has boomed. He takes care of the accounts and finances while I work... *worked* to extend our distribution to other states." Samuel padded over to Renee's lap and curled up on her thighs. "It will take time to refer to myself in the past tense."

Renee crooned over him and stroked his head.

"Though, this is not so bad," he murmured.

"How was your relationship with Mr. Albrecht?" Ophelia asked.

"Fine, as far as I know. Both a business partner and a good friend. He'll be at the office now, I'm sure. He always said we'd work ourselves to death," Samuel replied.

Ophelia nodded. While Samuel's statements painted a clearer picture, it was still unclear whose motive was the most powerful. It was time to meet Mr. Albrecht and check their alibis. "I appreciate your help, Mr. Quentin, and yours, Renee."

"I don't believe I was much help in these circumstances, but I am glad to assist, as always." Renee beamed.

"*Absurdité. Vous êtes un ange,*" Samuel purred while she scratched his head.

"Ahaha. *Merci,*" Renee replied.

Ophelia wanted to ask Renee how to get her cat back, but that could come later. First, she wanted to head to the offices of *Artisanal Aromas.*

5

Edward Albrecht was Samuel Quentin's age, but you would never know just by looking at him. He had tanned skin, a strong jawline, blonde hair, and bright green eyes. He stood nearly a head taller than Ophelia and was fit as a fiddle. He could have been Buster Crabbe's distant cousin.

They stood in the lobby of the *Artisanal Aromas* factory, where a security guard had checked her in and called on Edward to meet her.

After short introductions, Ophelia remarked, "I'm surprised you're open today."

"It's been chaos all morning, Ms. Windsor," Edward said, running a hand through his perfectly styled hair. "We're all so broken up over the news of Sam's death. I've sent most of the factory workers home; we're down to the skeleton crew today."

"I'm sorry for your loss, Mr. Albrecht." Large, framed photos of Samuel and Edward hung alongside awards and certificates from around the world. Enlarged magazine advertisements peppered the space between, hovering above the two velvet sofas placed for the factory's visitors. Ophelia took note of them as she readied her pad. "I'll do my best to keep this brief. Where were you last night after five p.m.?"

"I stayed late. Sam was here until around six, but the books always take extra time, as I'm sure you know."

"The books, meaning you handle the accounting?"

"I do. I have an accountant who checks them off once a month, but she's not as intimately familiar with them as I am."

"Her name, please?"

"Oh. Tabitha Jones."

Ophelia scribbled down the accountant's name. "Did you go anywhere after work last night?"

"Nah. I have a lady waiting at home. I turned in around eleven."

Ophelia raised an eyebrow. "You stayed here until eleven o'clock?"

"Well, no. I honestly don't remember what time I left. Eleven sticks out because that's what time I set my alarm."

The offices were a fifteen-minute cab ride from the Quentin's estate. Even if Edward lived an hour away, that was five hours unaccounted for. *That's plenty of time to commit a murder.* "Can someone here confirm the time you left?"

Edward smiled and shook his head. "First one through the door and last one to leave. My father raised me to be a businessman, I'm afraid."

"I take it yesterday wasn't Ms. Jones's monthly check-in?"

Edward chuckled. "No, I'm afraid not."

Ophelia nodded. "Do you and Mr. Quentin have equal shares in this business, Mr. Albrecht?"

"Absolutely. Fifty-fifty, that's how it's always been. As far as I understand it, his shares will now go to his wife."

Interesting. "Were any of the employees unhappy with Mr. Quentin or their positions here?"

Edward shook his head. "We pay a fair wage and offer better benefits than any other factory in Cicero. If someone was upset, I'm afraid that it escaped my notice."

"I see. Do you mind if I take a look through Mr. Quentin's office?"

"Not at all. This way, Ms. Windsor."

They passed by a small break room and a series of offices before Edward stopped outside a door with Samuel's name listed on a plate.

Edward opened the door, his charming smile still plastered on his face. "Anything else you need from me, you just holler."

"I'll do just that. Thank you, Mr. Albrecht."

Ophelia began her search in Samuel's desk drawers. Beyond a few personal banknotes, prescription receipts, and ancient invoices in the drawers' recesses, there was little else of interest. Two wooden shelves perched on the walls, filled from one end to the other with books covering business law, successful money-making tactics, and one novel that Ophelia couldn't make the name out it had been handled so often. Edward checked in on her once, but she kept to herself, checking for hidden compartments or secret drawers. At every turn, she found nothing.

The place was squeaky clean.

She lifted the receiver on Samuel's desk and dug Donald Frisbe's card from her pocket, along with her notebook. It was time to check in. He answered on the second ring.

"Detective Frisbe. It's Ophelia Windsor," Ophelia said.

"Ms. Windsor, I'm glad you called. Any progress?"

"Nothing substantial, I'm afraid. A troubled marriage and a familial relationship with his personal assistant, but nothing that points to murder," she sighed. "I'm at the *Artisanal Aromas* factory right now. Edward Albrecht carries himself like a movie star. Since

Samuel's business shares will go to his wife, it would seem that the lens turns back to her."

"Well, maybe this will help. The autopsy results came back—Samuel died of heart failure."

Ophelia sank into Samuel's chair. "So, that's it, then?"

"Not quite. The blood panels we ran showed an unusually high amount of digoxin."

Ophelia flipped to a blank page in her notepad. "Spell that for me?" *Digoxin.* "And what is that for?"

"It's generally used to treat heart arrhythmia. But too much can lead to heart failure."

"And the number fell into that 'too much' category?"

"Far too much."

"Were you able to speak with his physicians? Was that a pill he took daily?"

"It was. His cardiologist prescribed it for him but at a safe dosage."

"Is there a brand that I should keep an eye out for, Detective Frisbe? Of this digoxin?"

"Ah. Right. Lanoxin."

"Thank you." Ophelia jotted down the name and underlined it in her notebook.

Detective Frisbe paused, and the sound of pages turning followed. "I have the rest of his scripts here for you, but I think this is the one we need to focus on."

"Go ahead and give them to me anyway. Just in case."

Detective Frisbe listed ten more medications, slowly spelling them out for her. Ophelia had never heard of nine of them; the tenth she'd seen as a treatment for anxiety.

"And none of these could have had a fatal interaction?" she asked, marveling at the list.

"According to the three doctors I spoke with, they should all have been fine together."

"Alright." Ophelia flipped back to Victoria's notes. "Can I have you look up a flight number for me? I need to know when it arrived and if Victoria LaCoste was a passenger."

"Absolutely. Anything I can do to help."

Ophelia gave him the flight information and placed a dark checkmark next to it.

"Detective Frisbe? What are you still doing here?" Jackson's booming voice sounded from the other end of the line.

"Following up on a few leads, sir," Donald called.

"I'll call you later, Detective. Thank you." Ophelia hung up. No reason to keep him on the phone longer than necessary with Jackson nearby.

She leaned back in her chair and glanced around the office. If Edward had been the one to commit the crime, he'd done a great job cleaning up after himself.

In Samuel's office, at least.

Ophelia replaced the final stack of papers where she'd found it in Samuel's desk, then searched for Mr. Albrecht.

Edward's office was just a few steps away, his name emblazoned on a similar plaque to Samuel's. The door was cracked open a few inches; just enough for Ophelia to catch Edward's silhouette at his desk. She knocked twice and waited.

"Come on in, Ms. Windsor."

Ophelia stepped over the threshold and furrowed her brow. "You were expecting me?"

Edward grinned and shrugged. "I expected you wouldn't find what you were looking for."

Spoken like a man with something to hide. Was he toying with her? His demeanor prickled the tiny hairs on the back of her neck. "Would you mind terribly if I had a look through your books, Mr. Albrecht?"

His smile faltered for a split second. She watched the cogs spin in his expression. To decline her outright would sound like a confession. Offer too readily, and he could appear just as guilty. Especially if he took that worn leather journal cradled between his hands out of the room.

"You said you're a private investigator?"

"I did. I would be happy to negotiate a search warrant if that's what you prefer. However, the press is always eager to pick up on a new company scandal." Search warrants typically had a gag order, and if Edward called the precinct to test her fib, she would never hear the end of it. But she needed an in—she couldn't give him more time to destroy evidence.

Thankfully, the threat seemed to work. Edward's face paled and nodded. "There will be no need for that, Ms. Windsor." He set the journal on his desk, lifted his arms as if she had a gun pointed at him, and stepped away from the office. "I'll be inside the factory if you need anything else. It's the door at the end of the hall."

"Thank you, Mr. Albrecht." She watched him walk away and caught the sharp glance he awarded her from the corner of his eye.

What are you hiding, Edward?

Once she was alone, she set to work. First, the journal. She flipped it open to find scrawled dates and a few notes here and there on what needed to be ordered for the factory or dates when Edward or Samuel were out of town.

Then, tucked away in the back, was a two-page spread of a series of numbers and letters. Almost like a meticulously crafted bingo card. No matter how long she stared at it, she couldn't make sense of the jumbled numerals. She set the journal aside with a frown and peered around his office.

Two bookcases were filled to the brim with ledgers, forms, and paperwork. His desk drawers were neatly organized with pens, clean sheets of paper, and typical office supplies. She started with the ledgers.

Even in her few hundred years of being alive, Ophelia hadn't gained a firm grasp on accounting. Renee had attempted to teach her a few times, but the numbers and formulas always seemed to blur together in one chaotic whirlwind. The High Sorceress had at least managed to teach her the basics, and Ophelia clung to them now.

As she sorted through the last year's earnings and payments, she noticed tiny letters marked in the margins. None of them matched the account or product names, nor did they spell any coherent word when she slid her finger from the top of the page to the bottom, then in reverse.

Wait.

Ophelia's eyes widened. She snatched the small leather journal from his desk and flipped to the puzzling bingo page. Holding the journal next to the ledger, she combed over it again with her pen.

W: 100: R. 28. X: 46.

She returned to the weekly accounts and painstakingly did the math herself. She'd been wrong; paperwork wasn't her least favorite activity. It was accounting.

Even so, Renee's lessons paid off. As she finished her calculations, she realized that the final number Edward had written in the net income column was off by exactly the amount indicated by that week's letter. A hundred dollars the first week, twenty-eight the second, forty-six the third… The pages and tiny letters continued on until that current week's accounts. She flipped to the beginning of the year's ledger and found the same letter markings inside the margins. They were echoed throughout every ledger that Edward kept in his office.

Tens of thousands of dollars were unaccounted for, and every single week had Ms. Jones's signature of approval.

"And where is this money going, Mr. Albrecht?" Ophelia mused as she peered over the large stack on the floor. Embezzlement. That was one heck of a motive. If Samuel had discovered that Edward was stealing money from their company, she imagined Samuel would have been furious.

Ophelia pocketed the leather journal and held tight to one of the ledgers. If Edward tried anything drastic, she wanted to keep at least two pieces of evidence on her person. Having his bank records subpoenaed would be her next battle.

Before leaving the office, she murmured, "*Ecruli*," tapping three fingers to her left shoulder, then her right. A shimmering haze rippled from her head to her shoes. If Edward carried a gun, it would offer her a chance to respond.

Ophelia hurried down the hallway to the door he'd described and opened it to find a man sitting at a station filled with at least thirty dark bottles. He held an eyedropper in one hand and a bottle in the other, glancing over his shoulder to peer at Ophelia through thick goggles.

"Ma'am, this area is for employees only," he flatly advised.

"I understand. I'm a private investigator, and I need to find Edward Albrecht immediately. He told me he would be here."

The man turned back to face his bottles and shrugged. "I haven't seen him in a few hours, ma'am."

Ophelia quietly cursed beneath her breath, then rushed back down the hallway to the lobby. The security guard had his heavy lids fixed on a single monitor and his arms crossed.

"Did Mr. Albrecht come through here?" Ophelia asked.

The security guard cocked his head, then nodded. "He said he was heading home for the day, Ms. Windsor. Didn't he tell you?"

Ophelia shook her head. "Can you please give me his address? I need to ask him a few questions."

"Well, erm, I don't know if I'm of the authority to do that, Ms—"

"Will you give it to the police?" Ophelia was desperate.

"Oh. Well, then, yes, of course."

"Great. Can I use your phone?"

The guard slid the telephone as far as the cord would allow. Ophelia repositioned the ledger in her arm and snatched the receiver, quickly punching in the numbers to the police station.

"Lieutenant Jackson, please."

The wait felt cruel, and her heart raced. The guard exchanged worried glances between the monitor and Ophelia's face. At last, Jackson answered.

"Ophelia? What on Earth do you think you and Frisbe are doing?"

"Jackson, I need you to bring Edward Albrecht in for questioning immediately. I believe he'll leave town if we give him any more time."

The quiet, icy anger that Jackson reserved for Ophelia when she crossed the line coated his words like a thin film. "I should detain you both."

Not even *Ecruli* would spare her from his rage. "Please, Jackson. Felony embezzlement and possible murder. This kind gentleman at *Artisanal Aromas* will give you his address right now."

"Ophelia!"

She handed the guard the phone with a nod. They didn't have time to argue.

"Y-yes. Hello, s-sir." The guard stammered. He hesitated, then relayed Edward's home address just as Ophelia exited the building.

Max was off for the day, but the factory was on a busy road, and Ophelia managed to hail a cab to the police station quickly. As they swerved through the afternoon traffic, she wished she could summon the wind to speed the police's arrest. Every second Jackson spent deliberating over whether to agree with her was another second that Edward could put distance between them. She had to solve this case. For Samuel.

They arrived, and she generously tipped the driver before ascending the concrete steps to the station. Jackson was waiting for her at the check-in area.

"Is he here—" Ophelia began.

"Your evidence had better be *infallible,* Ophelia," Jackson growled. "Do you understand what's at stake?"

"I do." Jackson's superiors could very well fire him for trusting the word of a private investigator. Detective Frisbe's position was also compromised. However, she understood that neither of them should offer those suggestions in the presence of others. "Here." She offered him the ledger and the journal. "There are dozens of other books like this back at the factory. Mr. Albrecht stole thousands of dollars from his associate, then ran when I searched his office."

Jackson accepted the books, his dark, furious eyes unwavering on Ophelia's face. "He's in interrogation." He exhaled hard through his nostrils—Ophelia had escaped the bull's horns. For now. "Don't screw this up."

"Yes, sir."

Ophelia followed the familiar path to the interrogation room. Detective Frisbe stood outside the two-way glass, studying its inhabitant.

"Mind if I listen in?" he asked.

"By all means, Detective." Ophelia preferred this new side of Donald. Maybe he wasn't so bad to work with after all.

She entered the room and took a seat across from Edward Albrecht.

He looked up at her and flashed a movie-star smile. "Would you believe me if I told you I had a family emergency?"

"How long have you been stealing money from Mr. Quentin?" Ophelia asked. "Since the factory opened?"

"Stealing? I wouldn't imagine doing such a thing."

"Then please explain the cipher in your notebook to me."

Edward shrugged. "A game I play with my son. I write a letter; he writes a number."

"And that's how much money you decide to take that week?" Ophelia clasped her hands on the table. "Three of the weeks I calculated matched the amount missing in your cipher, Mr. Albrecht. Now, I may not be your accountant, but I believe when we check your and Ms. Jones's accounts, we'll find deposits that align with these differences."

Edward rolled his eyes. "Alright. We can play this straight. I stashed a little away for a rainy day. So what?"

"So Samuel found out that you'd taken thousands of dollars away from him, and you didn't like that."

"Wait, you don't think I killed him?" Edward's back straightened, and he squared his shoulders. "Where did this come from?"

"There's a lot of money missing, Mr. Albrecht. I've seen people kill for far less." She flipped open her notebook. "You had at least five hours of free time last night to visit Mr. Quentin in his home. Slip a few pills into his drink and leave quietly. No one would have questioned a visit from his business partner."

"Look, Ms. Windsor. I don't know if you found your badge in a box of Cracker Jacks, but you do not have the evidence to book me on murder. Because I didn't. Kill. Sam."

Ophelia brushed a strand of hair behind her ear, brushing his comment away with it. "I plan to do one more sweep of Mr. Quentin's estate. Enough fingerprints and an empty bottle would be enough to convince a judge, Mr. Albrecht."

"I want a lawyer," Edward snapped.

"You want to turn this into a circus? Spend a few nights behind bars? We can end this right now. Maybe earn you a reduced sentence if you play your cards right." That would be Detective Frisbe's field of expertise, but she knew how the game worked.

"And maybe they should get a real detective in here next time. I'm done talking."

Ophelia left the room to find Detective Frisbe chewing on his thumbnail.

"Thoughts?"

"I don't know if he did it," Donald admitted. "The embezzlement, sure. But I think he's telling the truth about Samuel."

"Mm. You may be right." Ophelia peeked down the hall. Jackson was gone, but his office door was slightly open. He was listening. Ophelia lowered her voice. "Well, as I said to Mr. Albrecht, I want to check the Quentins' one last time. Did you find out Victoria's flight information for me?"

"Still waiting on a call back from the airport."

"I'll call you later, then." She glanced over her shoulder, then whispered. "Do you need to drop this case, Detective?"

Donald shook his head. "You're tough as nails, Ms. Windsor. I'll try to stay the same."

"Very good." Ophelia smiled. "Now, if you would kindly cover for me."

Detective Frisbe offered a stark salute. Ophelia marched down the hallway, ignoring Jackson's stern voice as he called her name.

6

Ophelia didn't mind the quiet ride back to the mansion. The weather was cool, and the sun continued its gradual descent on the horizon. She worked to push away the colorful words Jackson would most assuredly have for her back at the station. There was a lot riding on this case.

But, if she was lucky, she could end her investigation here.

A young housekeeper still in her late teens answered the door. Her ginger hair was tied back in a braid, and freckles danced across her face as she spoke. She wore a black dress and a white apron—a standard from what Ophelia had seen from the others.

"Hello. I'm Ophelia Windsor, a private investigator. I was here earlier today, looking into Mr. Quentin's death."

"Oh. I heard Mrs. Quentin talking about that. What happened is so awful." She shifted her weight from one foot to the other. "How can I help you, ma'am?"

Ophelia readied her notebook. "I was hoping you could answer a few questions for me, actually, Ms…?"

"I'm Caitlin Moore, ma'am." Caitlin curtsied, then stepped out onto the front porch and closed the door behind her. "How can I help you?"

"Thank you, Ms. Moore. Have you worked here long?"

"About two years now."

"Always during the evenings?"

"Yes, I attend school during the day. The Quentins were kind enough to accommodate me."

"Were you working last night?"

"Yes, ma'am."

"Did the Quentins have any visitors?" Ophelia prepped her pen and held her breath.

"Only one, I believe. But I didn't answer the door. Mr. Quentin did." Caitlin blushed. "I heard a familiar voice, though. It sounded an awful lot like Ms. LaCoste, but I thought she was visiting with her mother."

Ophelia hesitated. "Did everyone in the house know about Ms. LaCoste's being out of town?"

"Yes. All of us were instructed to treat her as a member of the family. Not knowing the schedules of Mr. and Mrs. Quentin or Ms. LaCoste's can end in losing your job."

She lied about her flight... "Any particular reason you can think of that she would have visited last night?"

"She was very loyal to keeping Mr. Quentin up to date on her schedule. She always has her nose stuck in her planner. I'm sure it was to tell him that she'd returned and prepare him for the week." Caitlin shrugged. "We aren't told much about their personal lives, I'm afraid."

Ophelia nodded and made a note on Victoria's flight. She still had Edward's loose threads to tie up.

"Are you familiar with one Edward Albrecht?"

"Mr. Quentin's business partner? Oh yes. He's quite charming." Caitlin giggled. "He always brings the evening staff gifts when he goes on trips."

Ophelia wondered if it was Edward's money or Samuel's that was spent. "And you're certain he didn't stop by last night?"

"Not unless Mr. or Mrs. Quentin welcomed him in without me." She worried at the fabric of her apron. "But... I got an earful for not hearing the first ring last night."

Ophelia tapped the pen to her notepad. Edward was sliding down her short list of suspects. Any visit later than dinner time would have surely alerted Caitlin to his presence.

Ophelia decided to take another angle. There was one more suspect that needed further investigating. "How was Mr. and Mrs. Quentin's relationship?" She kept her expression carefully blank. Leading Caitlin to say what she wanted wouldn't hold up well in court.

"Well, u-um, what do you mean?"

Ophelia licked her lips. It was a careful dance to avoid leading questions. "How do they treat you and the other members of the staff?"

"T-they're very kind, ma'am. They did their best, I think. They… they, um…" Caitlin looked to the left, then the right. She bunched her apron up in her hands, and her cheeks turned red. "I'm sorry, I hate to be a gossip."

"I assure you, you are not. They what? Did something happen?"

Caitlin searched Ophelia's face for the span of a few heartbeats, then nodded. "Ever since Mrs. Quentin filed for divorce, they fought almost every day. Two nights ago, I—I heard Mrs. Quentin threaten him."

"What did she say?"

"That Mr. Quentin needed to give her a fair share of his money, or there would be, um, consequences." A thin sheen of sweat beaded on Caitlin's brow. "She didn't elaborate, ma'am."

Ophelia jotted down Clara's threat in her notebook. "Ms. Moore, do you know who has all access to Mr. Quentin's medication?"

The tension in Caitlin's shoulders eased a few inches. "Those are in his office. Mr. Quentin asked all of us to refill his pillbox at least once." She laughed uncomfortably. "I think we all know his daily pills by heart."

"Is Lanoxin one of those pills?"

"Oh. Yes. Why do you ask?"

"It's very important to this case. Would you mind showing me his prescriptions, Ms. Moore?"

Caitlin glanced over her shoulder. "Mrs. Quentin made it very clear that she didn't want any more police in the house today."

"But I'm not with the police," Ophelia quipped with a smile. When Caitlin's unease remained, she donned a more serious tone. "That medication is the heart of my investigation. I want to help close this case on Samuel Quentin, Ms. Moore. I think he deserves that. Don't you?"

Caitlin shuffled between her feet and chewed her lower lip. "O-okay. For Mr. Quentin. Let's just be quiet?"

"Silent as the grave," Ophelia assured her.

They moved silently through the foyer, down the hallway, and into Samuel's dark office. Caitlin flipped on the lights and closed the door behind them.

"His pillbox is right over here, Ms. Windsor," Caitlin whispered and tiptoed to the mahogany desk. She slid the top drawer out and moved to touch its contents.

"My apologies, Ms. Moore, but do you have a pair of gloves?" Ophelia slid her own gloves from her coat pocket. "We need to keep it free from fingerprints."

"Ah. Right. I'm sorry." Caitlin retrieved a pair of gloves from her apron before leaning back over the desk. "Here we are." She lifted a box with gold filigree and green gems embedded into its lid and then set it on top of the desk. "There are enough spaces for seven days," she explained as she lifted the lid. "And he keeps his medications in the same drawer."

Ophelia peered over Caitlin's shoulder and glimpsed eleven prescription bottles laying neatly in the top drawer.

"Since it's Tuesday, he would have—...hm. That's strange." Caitlin leaned forward and inspected the box's contents.

"What is?"

Caitlin shifted a stack of colored pills aside, revealing a cluster of tiny white pills. "Well, this pill here. He's only supposed to have one of these a day." She pushed through the other days with her gloved finger, brushing the top pills away. "Someone put six of these in each slot, with five other pills on top to hide them."

"Who last refilled his pill case for the week?"

"W-well, I did. But I would never dream of—"

Ophelia held up a hand. "It's alright, Ms. Moore. I don't believe it was you." She went to the desk and searched through multiple pill bottles. The 'Lanoxin' bottle was missing.

Caitlin blinked, and her mouth formed a tiny 'o' of surprise. "He would have taken six today, too! Is that what happened, Ms. Windsor? Did he take all of those pills?"

"It seems so." It was a vain hope, but Ophelia looked around the desk and in the small trash can at its base for the bottle. "Ms. Moore, could you watch the door a moment? I'd like to make a phone call." The last thing she wanted was for Clara to find them in Samuel's office together.

"Of course, Ms. Windsor. I'll be right outside," Caitlin said, then vanished behind the door.

Ophelia's mind spun as she reconsidered every aspect of the case. The pill box could be dusted for prints, but if everyone in the house had handled the box at some point, then everyone's prints would be there.

Motive. Motive. Motive...

Clara wasn't getting what she wanted in the divorce. With Samuel dead, the company shares would be hers, his fortunes would be hers, and if he had a life insurance policy, that would also be hers.

Following that path, why didn't Clara reset his pills? Even if she'd disposed of the bottle, she'd been home all day and had ample opportunity to reset Samuel's medications to appear as they normally would. Such an obvious blunder would lose her all claims to the life insurance and their shared property.

Edward was slowly collecting money from the company. With enough saved, a quiet escape and concurrent shutdown of the perfume giant would allow him to sell his shares without fear of his embezzlement coming to light.

However, it seemed that Samuel truly had no idea of Edward's betrayal. Besides, Caitlin had confirmed that Edward wasn't in the house the night prior, and Ophelia's theory of spiking Samuel's drink had died with the discovery that every day of his pills was tampered with.

That left Victoria. She was in the will and most likely on Samuel's life insurance policy. But her motive felt the most conflicted. It seemed Samuel treated her like family—both from Samuel's testimony and from Caitlin's. What did she have to gain?

Clara. Victoria. Edward. Clara. Victoria. Edward.

Ophelia picked up the phone and dialed Donald Frisbe. He answered on the first ring.

"Ms. Windsor? Is that you?"

"Yes. Is Lieutenant Jackson watching you like a hawk?"

There was a pause. "Yes."

"Then I'll make this brief. Did you hear from the airport?"

"I did. They confirmed that Victoria LaCoste was on the flight you gave me. It returned Sunday morning at eleven o'clock."

"Two days ago?"

"Correct."

Victoria. "I'm going to need a favor."

"Name it."

"Convince Lieutenant Jackson to bring in Victoria LaCoste for questioning."

Donald's grimace was palpable. "Name something else."

"Tough as nails?"

The detective grunted his displeasure.

"I'm sorry, Detective Frisbe. I'll meet you at the station."

"Make sure you put an application for my job while you're here, Ms. Windsor." Detective Frisbe replied, followed by a soft click.

Ophelia rushed out of the office. "Caitlin, I need to take the pillbox and medications with me, please."

"W-why?" Caitlin squeaked.

"I believe we're about to catch a murderer."

Lieutenant Simon Jackson stood straight-backed, using all six-plus feet of his height to his advantage, waiting for the second time that day at the station's check-in for Ophelia.

"For your second act, you have me haul in a crying, unsuspecting young woman, and you show up in my police station with your *cat*?" Jackson hissed.

"Meow?" To Samuel's credit, it sounded very much like Figaro.

"It's complicated," Ophelia countered, shifting Samuel in one arm and the box of pills in the other. "Where's Victoria?"

"Detective Frisbe can show you, seeing as you two decided to play *Bobbsey Twins* on this case." Before Ophelia could take a step, Jackson gripped her shoulder. "This is it, Ophelia. Finish it now, or I'm detaining you for the next three days while I clean up your mess."

"Yes, sir."

"Detective Frisbe will join you while he enjoys an extensive review of his career," Jackson continued. "If you're wrong, you can say goodbye to your ties with this station."

Ophelia's fingers and toes went numb. Samuel's tail twitched nervously against her arm. She steeled herself. "I understand, Jackson."

"Go."

Detective Frisbe nervously ushered her around the furious lieutenant, and Ophelia rushed to join him. Murmurs of obstinant disobedience reached her ears as Jackson followed behind them.

"Did you have to bring the cat?" Donald whispered.

"It's complicated," Ophelia repeated.

A tearful Victoria awaited them in one of the interrogation rooms. Just Ophelia entered, but she knew Detective Frisbe and Lieutenant Jackson would be watching her very closely on the other side of that glass.

"I-I don't understand. What is this?" Victoria stammered. "Is that a cat?"

"You lied to me, Victoria," Ophelia said, setting Samuel down on the table. He sat back and silently observed Victoria's face.

"What do you mean?"

"You told me that you came home from your trip this morning. We confirmed that it returned on Sunday."

"Is that seriously why you arrested me? Because I have my days mixed up?" Victoria snapped.

"I find that incredibly difficult to believe. You carry your planner on you at all times, don't you? When I spoke with you earlier, you seemed ready to give me exact dates and times on almost everything."

Samuel nodded. Ophelia hoped Victoria didn't see.

"My mom is *sick*, Ms. Windsor. Time feels like a blur some days. Is that so farfetched?"

"Maybe not." Ophelia carefully slid the pillbox from the bag. "Tell me, did you take care of Mr. Quentin's pills for this week?" She knew Caitlin had set them, but she hoped to slowly work a confession from Victoria.

"I was out of town!" Victoria's face blanched as she looked at the glittering box. "I-I... I thought one of the housekeepers did. Caitlin or Beverly?"

"Well, since you were home yesterday, Ms. LaCoste, I thought you may have done the honors. And I'm betting if I dust all of these for prints, I'll find yours on this box."

"*Everyone* filled Sam's pillbox at some point. You'll find my prints, the housekeepers', Clara's, and Sam's on both!" She shook her head. "I told you already! I didn't return to work until this morning."

"You did. But Ms. Moore says you visited Mr. Quentin last night."

Samuel tipped his head and flicked his tail. Apparently, that particular memory had vanished alongside the one of his death.

Victoria chewed her lip and looked from Samuel to Ophelia. "I still don't understand why you brought the cat…. This is such a sham—"

"Why did you visit Mr. Quentin last night, Ms. LaCoste?"

"Like I said. My mother is sick. My days were off, and he deserved to know that I was back early."

"How long did you stay for?"

"I…" Victoria stuttered and flushed. "I was only there for half an hour. Maybe an hour."

"Enough time to replace his pills with Lanoxin?"

"Excuse me?" She flinched, and a thin sheen of sweat formed across her skin like a veil.

"His daily medications were replaced with Lanoxin. Or digoxin, as it's more commonly known." Ophelia tapped her notebook. "Even Caitlin recognized the fatal consequences of an overdose. Certainly, you must have known."

Anger flared in Victoria's eyes. "Well, yes. If you take six of *any* of his pills, it could be fatal."

"I didn't say how many were replaced," Ophelia replied quietly.

Samuel bared his teeth and hissed.

The anger vanished, and Victoria's face fell. Tears pooled in her eyes, and she sniffed.

"If I dust the Lanoxin bottle for recent prints, will I find yours, Ms. LaCoste?"

"But I...I threw it away..." The tears fell free, and Victoria gasped for air. "I... Oh, Sam..."

Ophelia pressed on. "Why did you kill him, Victoria?"

Victoria choked back sobs and covered her eyes with her hand. "My mom. My mom is so sick, Ms. Windsor. There's a surgery that could save her, but there was no way I could afford it. I asked Sam for help, but with the divorce, he said he might lose everything."

"But you're in Mr. Quentin's will," Ophelia said.

"Yes. I'm in the will." Victoria coughed before continuing. "I-if the will was paid out before the divorce was finalized, I would have enough for the procedure. I could save my mom." She covered her face with both hands.

"She's all I have left. God, I'm so sorry, Sam. I'm so, so sorry."

Detective Frisbe and Lieutenant Jackson entered the room, handing her a confession to sign while Detective Frisbe read Victoria her rights. Jackson's rage had calmed, but the look on his face said they were absolutely going to talk later.

Samuel's shoulders sank, and he hopped off the table into Ophelia's lap.

"I know," Ophelia whispered and scratched him behind the ears. "I know."

Renee and Ophelia sat in her apartment's living room, sharing the sofa with Samuel on Renee's lap.

"Should I have done more?" Samuel asked.

"No, sweet. You did all you could for Victoria," Renee replied.

Ophelia agreed. "Shc made the wrong decision, Mr. Quentin, not you."

Samuel nodded, then sat up. "So, then. What do we do now?"

"Now, *mon cher ami*, I put you to sleep. Your spirit will continue on its journey into the beyond." Renee stroked his head. "I sense you've found your resolution here, but there is so much more waiting for you."

"Not an endless eternity in limbo?" Samuel curled his tail around his paws.

"No. I can promise you that."

"That's reassuring." Samuel pawed his way into Ophelia's lap. "I suppose I should thank you both. And please thank Detective Frisbe for hiring you, Ms. Windsor. I know the circumstances are… strange, but I am glad to know the truth."

"You're welcome, Mr. Quentin." Ophelia offered him a few more head scratches.

"Ophelia is simply the best at what she does," Renee praised. "You'll not find any like her."

"I see that. It was a pleasure being your housecat." Samuel smiled, though it looked strange on a cat's face. "I guess that I will see you on the other side."

"Sweet dreams, Samuel," Ophelia said.

Renee placed a hand on his head and murmured a long string of incantations. Samuel's eyelids drooped, and his body relaxed into a curled circle in Ophelia's lap. His breathing steadied, and he purred quietly as he fell asleep.

"Figaro will wake in the morning, darling. I'm certain his spirit is exhausted after fighting another's desires." Renee touched Ophelia's shoulder. "And you should get some well-deserved rest, too."

"I will in just a bit. Thank you, Renee."

"My pleasure, dear. I will call you in the morning. Through the mirror this time." She kissed Ophelia's cheek. "Sleep well, Ophelia."

"You, too."

After Renee left, Ophelia stroked Figaro's head and mused over the thought of him talking all of the time. Maybe it wouldn't be so bad.

Safe travels, Samuel.

THANK YOU FOR READING!

Thank you so much for reading the first novelette of *Ophelia P.I*! We hope you enjoyed this paranormal cozy mystery. If you think others would enjoy this book, please take a few moments, and leave a review on Amazon, Goodreads, Barnes & Noble, or Bookbub. You can't imagine how helpful this would be! We read each and every review to help us improve on our writing, as well as give us more ideas.

MEETING RENEE: A PREQUEL VIGNETTE

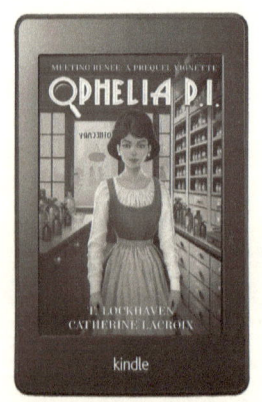

Download for free at: amz.run/9DjL

In the heart of 1660s New York lies an enchanting secret hidden within Ophelia Windsor's apothecary.

Ophelia harbors a magical talent that transcends mere potion brewing. When a mysterious stranger with profound magical prowess steps into her shop, he sets up a meeting for her with the High Sorceress, Renee Swan.

Have you read the first book in the main series of Ophelia P.I.? If you haven't, check it out! It precedes the short story.

There are three types of series for Ophelia P.I.: main series, novelettes, and short stories. You currently read the first short story. Check out the others for more cozy mysteries.

MAIN   SHORT   NOVELETTE

Follow authors T. Lockhaven and Catherine LaCroix on Amazon, Goodreads and Bookbub to receive notifications of their new releases. You may also sign up for T. Lockhaven's VIP newsletter at:

twistedkeypublishing.com/tlockhaven

Be sure to check out T. Lockhaven's other cozy mystery series.

MERRY AND MOODY WITCH COZY MYSTERIES

⇛ Book 1: Potion Commotion
⇛ Book 2: Bittersweet Deceit

COFFEE HOUSE SLEUTHS

⇛ Book 1: A Garden to Die For
⇛ Book 2: A Mummy to Die For
⇛ Christmas Book 1: Sleighed

www.ingramcontent.com/pod-product-compliance
Lightning Source LLC
Chambersburg PA
CBHW050426110726
47899CB00008B/2868